MARVEL
SPIDEY and his AMAZING FRIENDS

THE POWER OF THREE

Adapted by **Steve Behling**
Illustrated by **Premise Entertainment**

A GOLDEN BOOK • NEW YORK

MARVEL

© 2021 MARVEL

All rights reserved. Published in the United States by Golden Books, an imprint of Random House Children's Books, a division of Penguin Random House LLC, 1745 Broadway, New York, NY 10019, and in Canada by Penguin Random House Canada Limited, Toronto. Golden Books, A Golden Book, A Little Golden Book, the G colophon, and the distinctive gold spine are registered trademarks of Penguin Random House LLC.

rhcbooks.com

Educators and librarians, for a variety of teaching tools, visit us at RHTeachersLibrarians.com

ISBN 978-0-593-37933-2 (trade) — ISBN 978-0-593-37934-9 (ebook)

Printed in the United States of America

10 9 8 7 6

"Hey—that was my power-up, Miles!" Gwen said as she pressed the buttons on her game controller. She was at her friend Peter Parker's house, playing video games with him and another friend, Miles.

"Nope, I beat you to it!" Miles replied.

"Aha!" Peter said. "Bonus points! Now I'm winning!"
Just then, Peter's Aunt May poked her head into the room to say she was going to the store for ice cream.

"What flavor of ice cream would you like?" Aunt May asked.

"You know my favorite flavor," Peter replied. "**Cherry vanilla**, please!"

"Chocolate chip is my fave!" Gwen said.

"Mine is pistachio!" Miles added.

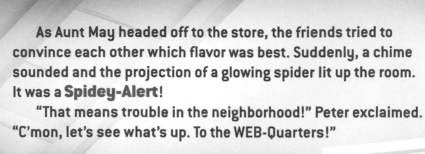

As Aunt May headed off to the store, the friends tried to convince each other which flavor was best. Suddenly, a chime sounded and the projection of a glowing spider lit up the room. It was a **Spidey-Alert**!

"That means trouble in the neighborhood!" Peter exclaimed. "C'mon, let's see what's up. To the WEB-Quarters!"

In a flash, Peter pulled a hidden lever. The friends jumped onto the slides that opened in Peter's closet. On the way down, they changed into their **Super Hero** costumes! In a snap . . .

Peter became Spidey!
Gwen became Ghost-Spider!
And Miles turned into Spin!

SPIDEY

SPIN

GHOST-SPIDER

They arrived at WEB-Quarters, their top-secret Spidey hideout. TRACE-E, a super-smart robot, was there to greet them.

"Hey, TRACE-E!" Spidey said. "What's up?"

As **TRACE-E** activated the computer, the horned villain known as Rhino lit up the view screen. Rhino liked to steal things—and ram into things!

"Looks like Rhino stole a big bag of gold from the bank," Ghost-Spider said.

The friends were ready to catch Rhino! But they couldn't agree on the best way to stop him. Spidey wanted to use his wall-crawling and web-slinging abilities, but his friends had other ideas.

"I can glide in with my super spider-powers," Ghost-Spider said.
"Rhino won't even see me coming when I use my Cloaking Power,"
Spin boasted as he became invisible.

Putting on their masks, the friends raced to the roof.

"Okay, **Spidey Team**!" Spidey shouted. "On three! One—"

But Ghost-Spider didn't want to wait. "Here I go!" she yelled, and swung away on her web!

Spin had already taken off, too.

"Hey, team! Wait for me!" Spidey called.

When the friends arrived at the bank, Spidey said,
"We need to track down Rhino. Let's look for some clues!"
"Check it out!" Spin replied. "A giant hole in the wall,
and Rhino-shaped footprints. Hard to miss these clues!"

"Those are good clues!" Ghost-Spider said from across the street.
"But I'm using my super detective skills, and I just found one of the
stolen coins! So maybe Rhino went that way?"

"Or this way!" Spin replied, pointing in the direction of the footprints.

"Only one way to find out," Spidey added. "We need a higher view!"

The heroes swung to the top of a building with their webs.
Through the special goggles in his high-tech mask, Spidey
saw Rhino getting away with the stolen coins.

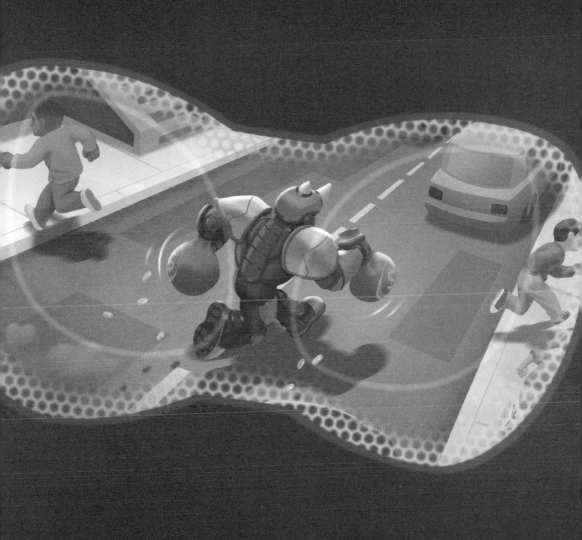

"Okay, here's the plan," Spidey told his friends. "What if we sneak up on Rhino and—" Before he could finish, Spin used his **Cloaking Power** to become invisible!

"Don't disappear yet!" Ghost-Spider said. "I've got a better way to sneak in. I'll use my web-wings and glide down quickly to web him!"

Spidey was starting to get annoyed. He wondered how they were going to catch Rhino if they couldn't all stick to the same plan.

Ghost-Spider swooped down on Rhino. As she quickly spun her web, she bumped into something—or someone! It was Spin! Ghost-Spider accidentally covered him in webbing. And at the same time, she got caught in his web!

HAR, HAR! THE LITTLE SPIDERS GOT STUCK IN EACH OTHER'S WEBS!

Still laughing, Rhino escaped. Ghost-Spider and Spin groaned.
"I let Rhino get away," Spin said. "I'm sorry."
"No, I'm pretty sure that was because of me," Ghost-Spider insisted.
"**We're a team**, remember?" Spidey said. "And that means working together, not arguing with each other."

Ghost-Spider and Spin realized that Spidey was right.

"We're going to need **all our powers** to stop Rhino," Spin said.
"Like your cool Gliding Power!"

"And your amazing Cloaking Power!" Ghost-Spider replied.

"Both of your powers are strong," Spidey told them. "But they're
even stronger when we stick together."

Now the Spidey Team was ready for action! With the help of TRACE-E, they located Rhino again. Then they put their plan into action. Spin was the first to swing in.

"You can't stop me, spider!" Rhino shouted. "So crawl back where you came from!"

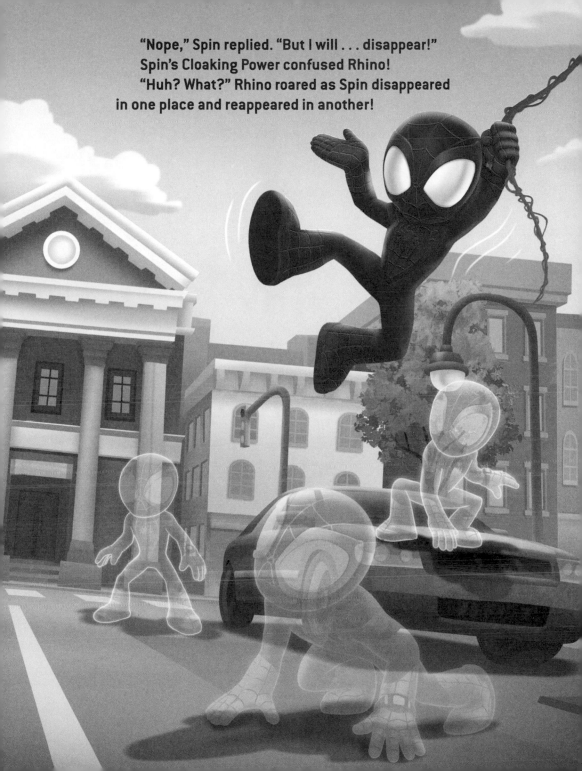

While Rhino was distracted by Spin, Spidey and Ghost-Spider got to work.
"Let me take that off your hands," Spidey said. He spun a web and pulled the bag of money away from Rhino!

Ghost-Spider soared in and webbed the villain's feet to the ground.
"Now you're stuck, Rhino!" Ghost-Spider said.

Rhino roared. Together, the heroes webbed
him and started to spin him around and around!

"I'm dizzy!" Rhino shouted. "Make it stop!"
"Sure, Rhino!" Spidey replied. "You're all
wrapped up and ready to go to jail!"

After stopping the Rhino, the Spidey Team raced home. They arrived at Peter's house just before Aunt May returned from the store.

"Who's ready for ice cream?" Aunt May asked merrily. "I have all your favorite flavors!"

"Thanks, Aunt May!" Peter said. Turning to his friends, he whispered, "And I bet these flavors work great together. Just like the **three of us**!"